© Aladdin Books Ltd 2001

Designed and produced by
Aladdin Books Ltd
28 Percy Street
London W1P 0LD

*First published in
the United States in 2001 by*
Copper Beech Books,
an imprint of
The Millbrook Press
2 Old New Milford Road
Brookfield, Connecticut 06804

ISBN 0-7613-2172-1

*Cataloging-in-Publication data is on
file at the Library of Congress*

Printed in Belgium
All rights reserved

Coordinator
Jim Pipe

Design
Flick, Book Design and Graphics

Picture Research
Brian Hunter Smart

My World

Can I Help?

by Dr. Alvin Granowsky

Copper Beech Books
Brookfield, Connecticut

balloons

2

Today is the big day.

It is the day of the barbecue!

"We all need to help," says Mom.
"I will help you tie up the
balloons, Sam."

tying the balloons

3

"Can I help?" asks Jenny.

"Yes," says Mom. "You can take the dog outside."

So Jenny takes the dog outside for a walk.

"Thank you for helping," says Mom.

the dog
outside

"Can I help?" asks Dad.

"Yes," says Mom.
"You can feed
the baby."

So Dad feeds
the baby.

**feeding
the baby**

What a big mess they make!

"Clean up the mess," says Mom, laughing.

"The others will be here soon."

Jenny looks at the mess in her room. Just then, Sasha and her mom arrive.

"Can I help?" asks Sasha.

toys in a mess

"Yes," says Jenny. "Please help me clean up my toys."

So Sasha helps Jenny. Soon the room is cleaned up.

Jenny's mom is busy cooking.
"Can I help?" asks Sasha's mom.

"Yes," says Jenny's mom. "You
can help me make a salad."

making
a salad

So Sasha's mom makes a salad.

salad

"Thank you," says Jenny's mom.

"That salad looks yummy."

"Can I help?" asks Sam.

"Yes," says Mom. "You can help Mrs. Lee carry her pie."

So Sam goes to Mrs. Lee's house.

a cherry pie

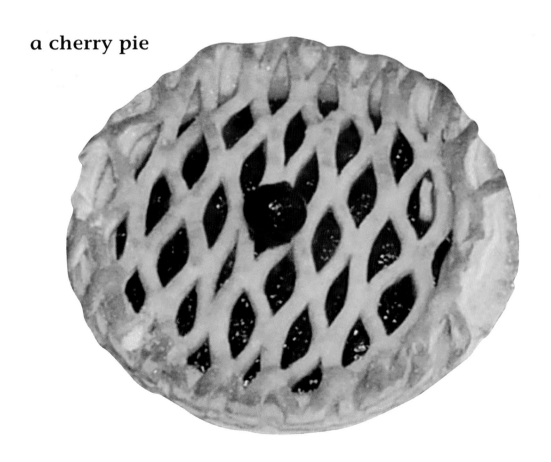

"Hi, Mrs. Lee," says Sam. "I can carry your pie to my house."

Sam carries the pie *very* slowly. He does not want to drop it.

carrying the pie

At Sam's house, Mrs. Lee says,
"Thank you, Sam."

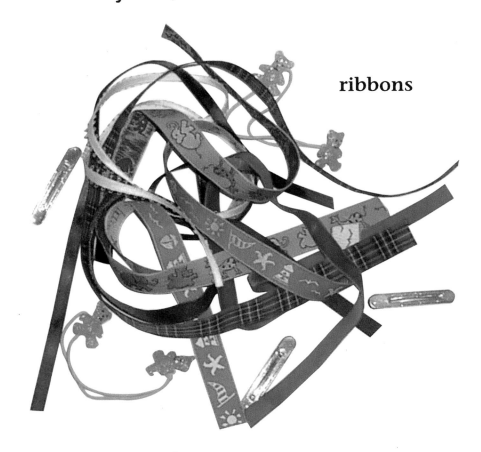

ribbons

Then she asks, "Can I help?"
"Yes," says Sasha. "Can you tie
ribbons in our hair?"

tying ribbons

So Mrs. Lee ties ribbons in
their hair.
"Thank you," say the two girls.

Outside, Dad is cooking
on the barbecue.

cooking on
the barbecue

"Can we help?" ask Jenny,
Sasha, and Sam.

"No, thanks," says Dad.
"Fires can be dangerous.
Ask Mom if she needs help."

"Can we help?" ask the children.

"Yes," says Mom. "You can carry everything outside."

carrying
the food
and cups

So the children carry out the bread, salad, plates, and cups.

Soon everything is on the table.

"The food is ready," says Dad.

"The table is ready, too," say Sam, Jenny, and Sasha.

the table and food are ready

"Thank you all for helping,"
says Mom.

"Now, please help yourselves!"

Here are some words and phrases from the book.

make a salad

cook the food

clean up the room

tie the balloons

tie the ribbons

feed the baby

carry the pie

take the dog outside

Can you use these words to
write your own story?

Did you see these in the book?

glasses

tomato

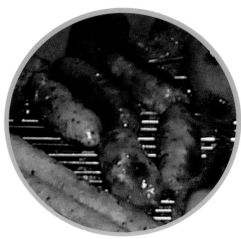

sausages

shoe

Illustrator: Mary Lonsdale for SGA

Picture credits:
All photographs supplied by Select Pictures